RUN DOWN

Rick Blechta

A PRATT & ELLIS MYSTERY

RAVEN BOOKS
an imprint of
ORCA BOOK PUBLISHERS

Library and Archives Canada Cataloguing in Publication

Blechta, Rick, author
Rundown / Rick Blechta.
(Rapid reads)

Issued also in print and electronic formats.
ISBN 978-1-4598-1010-5 (pbk.).—ISBN 978-1-4598-1011-2 (pdf).—
ISBN 978-1-4598-1012-9 (epub)

I. Title. II. Series: Rapid reads
PS8553.L3969R86 2016   C813'.54   C2016-900777-4
C2016-900778-2

First published in the United States, 2016
Library of Congress Control Number: 2016931823

Summary: In this work of crime fiction, two Toronto police detectives
investigate a series of hit-and-runs. (RL 3.4)

FSC
MIX
Paper from
responsible sources
FSC® C103214
www.fsc.org

*Orca Book Publishers is dedicated to preserving the environment and has
printed this book on Forest Stewardship Council® certified paper.*

Orca Book Publishers gratefully acknowledges the support for
its publishing programs provided by the following agencies:
the Government of Canada through the Canada Book Fund and the
Canada Council for the Arts, and the Province of British Columbia
through the BC Arts Council and the Book Publishing Tax Credit.

Cover design by Jenn Playford
Cover photography by Getty Images

ORCA BOOK PUBLISHERS
www.orcabook.com

Printed and bound in Canada.

19 18 17 16 • 4 3 2 1

ONE

Staff Inspector McDonnell stuck his head out of his office. The squad room was empty except for one desk. He sighed. This was going to be *very* unpopular.

"Pratt! I need to talk to you."

He watched the older detective's shoulders slump. Pratt should have left a half hour ago, but he only knew one way—do the job right. He needed to finish a report, period.

Mac returned to his office and read the email again.

Pratt said from the doorway, "I'm not going to like this, am I, Mac?"

"How do you know that?"

"The look on your face."

Mac knew Pratt could walk away from the job. Over the past year he'd seemed closer to finally retiring—yet he stayed on. Mac was grateful.

One thing Mac had got very right was to team Pratt with young Ellis. Under Pratt's watchful eye, Ellis was showing signs of someday being as good as his mentor—as long as he kept himself out of trouble. Come to think of it, Pratt wasn't good at that either.

"Mac?" Pratt prompted.

"Sorry. Too many things on my mind."

"It's that bad?"

McDonnell sighed. "We've got another one. Sit. Please."

Pratt moved a chair forward and heaved his bulk onto it. "You mean a hit-and-run ?"

Mac nodded. The first had taken place in downtown Toronto two weeks earlier.

A businessman had been struck and killed in a parking garage late at night. The car used had been stolen and later abandoned. Even though there was video of the crime, nothing useful had been learned from it. As a result, little progress had been made on the case. The victim had no known enemies, nothing in his life that would lead to murder.

"Details?" Pratt asked, taking out his flip notebook.

Mac spent about a minute running over what was known.

"So pretty much the same as the last one," he concluded. "Woman jogger this time, out with her dog in North Toronto. Hit from behind."

"Any witnesses?"

"Besides the dog?"

Pratt responded dryly, "Dogs usually don't make good witnesses."

Mac laughed, then grew serious. "They're not going to be happy upstairs, you know."

"When are they ever?"

"I need you to jump on this. This new victim wasn't killed, although she's gravely injured. We need to find out what happened—as soon as we can."

"Ellis?"

"I want him at the crime scene ASAP. You go to the hospital."

"He's at the movies with his wife."

"So?"

"He's already stood her up—twice."

Mac chuckled. He was on his third wife. "Then she shouldn't have married a cop."

Pratt got to his feet. "I'll send him a text."

"Keep me in the loop."

"Don't I always?"

"No, you don't," Mac said to himself after Pratt had left, "and someday that's really going to cost you."

TWO

Pratt wasn't as upset as he'd shown Mac outwardly. His big concern actually *was* his partner's wife. Ellis took his job seriously, perhaps too seriously, and left Jen alone far too often. It had actually been Pratt's idea that the couple have a "date night."

Now this. Obviously, it couldn't wait. With reluctance he picked up his cell phone and pressed the speed-dial key for Ellis.

Ellis didn't pick up. Maybe he'd turned off his cell phone—for once. Pratt's message was brief.

"Call me. Something's come up."

The call was returned seventy-three seconds later. "This had better be good. The movie just started."

Pratt sighed. "We've got another hit-and-run, very much like the one two weeks ago."

"Oh man…"

"If I could handle this alone for a few hours, I would, but I can't be in two places at once."

Now Ellis sighed. "Give me the details. I'll make Jen understand—somehow."

Ellis headed to the accident scene. Pratt got driven to Sunnybrook Hospital.

= = =

After exiting the elevator on the surgery floor, Pratt showed his identification to a tired-looking woman at the nursing station, telling her why he'd come.

The nurse stared at the badge. "Homicide? You don't waste time, do you? The patient isn't even dead yet."

He ignored the attempt at levity. "Can you bring me up to date?"

"There isn't much hope, but the surgical team is doing what it can."

"When will we know the outcome?"

The nurse shrugged. "I've been here long enough to know it doesn't look good."

"Was the victim conscious?"

That was greeted by a snort. "She was lucky to be breathing."

"Is there anyone waiting for news? Family? Husband? Boyfriend?"

"Husband. Darren Smith. Someone else is with him."

"Where do I find them?"

"Waiting room. Know where it is?"

The detective nodded. "Please find me the moment anything changes. Okay?"

He found four people in the waiting room. A couple was huddled miserably in the far corner. Closer to the door were two men. One was staring at the floor. The other was texting. They were turned away from each other.

"Which of you is Darren Smith?"

The one staring downward raised his hand without looking up.

"May I talk to you in the hall?" When the second man also rose, Pratt added, "Just Smith."

Away from the door, Pratt introduced himself, saying only that he was a detective, *not* a homicide detective.

"How much do you know about the accident your wife was involved in?"

Smith rubbed his face. "Only what the policeman who came to my office told me. Basically, where and when and that they'd brought Becky here."

"So you were still at work?"

"Yes. Rebecca always arrives home ahead of me. She takes the dog for a quick run. When I get there, we have a late dinner or go out."

"Does she always use the same route on her runs?"

"For her evening run with the dog, yes. Always the same."

"So where she was found doesn't surprise you?"

Smith shook his head. "The school is at the far end of her run. She always swings around the playground, then heads home." He looked up, despair on his face. "I want the bastard who did this caught and sent to prison."

"That's why I'm here. Next question. Who is your friend in the waiting room?"

"Curt? I work with him. He offered to come with me." Smith's shoulders slumped. "I can't take this."

"You're all close friends?"

"Not really. He knows Becky from university, that's all."

"I'm sorry to have imposed at this time. We can talk again later. Would that be all right?"

Smith shuffled back to the waiting room without answering.

THREE

The accident scene was alive with flashing lights and a crowd of gawkers. Snow was falling again. Early April, and still winter wouldn't let go of Toronto.

As usual, Ellis got stopped at the yellow perimeter tape. Everyone knew Pratt. Very few knew Ellis. He was challenged nearly every time, and it was annoying. Pratt joked it was because Ellis looked more like a reporter than a cop.

The sergeant finally raised the tape and let him through. Only after that did Ellis realize he should have done that himself in the first place—just walked in.

Let it roll off your back, he told himself.

Four techs had been sent to the crime scene. Since they were still working it up, Ellis couldn't get as close as he wanted. But he knew one of the techs and called him over.

"Hey, Stu! What can you tell me?"

"So the victim's dead?"

"Not as far as I've heard."

"Then why is homicide here?

"Luck of the draw. So tell me what you know."

"Our victim was running along the sidewalk by the schoolyard fence over there, apparently with her dog."

"Any witnesses?"

He shrugged. "Don't know. Talk to Sergeant Lewis over by the tape. He's got men going door to door."

They'd moved a bit closer to the action. Casts of tire tracks in some mud were being made. Stu began taking photos again, pointing out the dog's tracks next to the victim's.

Ellis stayed around for a few hours. The night was cold, and the wind made it feel worse. The scene was too big to cover it all with tents. Snow fell steadily. The crime scene techs had to work fast. Ellis wandered around, talking and using his eyes and cell-phone camera. By the time he packed it in for the night, he had a pretty good idea what had occurred.

Rebecca Smith hadn't stood a chance.

FOUR

Pratt updated Mac from the hospital.
"It's not looking good. I doubt I'm going
to get a chance to talk to the victim."

Mac wasn't happy. "That's a real shame."

Afterward Pratt stood in the hallway for
a moment. Should he grab something to
eat or go help Ellis?

He decided to give Ellis space. Let him
learn the ropes. Turning for the elevators,
he spotted the nurse he'd spoken to, with a
surgeon.

Stopping, he introduced himself. "Any
news?"

The surgeon sighed. "She didn't make it. Her injuries were too great."

"I appreciate your telling me."

"Not a problem. This next part won't be pleasant. Never is."

Pratt watched the surgeon enter the waiting room, shoulders slumped in defeat.

Pratt's grumbling stomach won out— even if dinner would be hospital food.

He swung into the food area just off the hospital's lobby. Since it was cold out, Pratt thought a stew-like offering might be worth trying.

Taking his tray to a table in the far corner, he sat and ate. And thought.

A few minutes later Darren Smith's friend appeared. Hesitating for a moment, he then joined the line for coffee. Pratt watched.

After paying, the man turned, looking for a seat. The detective caught his eye, motioning to him. The man's face as he walked over was unreadable.

As soon as he'd sat, Pratt asked, "So you know the news?"

The man nodded. "Tough on Darren. They were very close."

"I understand your name is Curt," Pratt said, sticking out his hand.

"Yeah. Curt Dewalt. I work with Darren."

"Why did you come down with him?"

"Loyalty. Sense of duty. He helped me get my job, actually."

Pratt took another spoonful of stew. "Do you know anything you think would be helpful?"

"What do you mean?"

"Well, sometimes people tell friends something they wouldn't or couldn't tell their spouse. You're what? Midthirties?"

"Thirty-seven. And no, I don't know anything. Darren and I don't socialize."

"What about you and his wife?"

Anger crossed his face, quickly suppressed. "He told you Rebecca and I knew each other in university? That's how I met Darren. And no, there was zilch going on between us."

Pratt nodded. "So Darren seemed normal lately?"

"I guess so."

"Can you think of anyone who'd want to harm Rebecca Smith?"

"This is crazy!" Dewalt said a bit too loudly. "Why would I know something like that?"

"It's part of my job to ask questions, find out what happened. You might know something. Small. A trifle. But it could help us catch the person who did this."

Dewalt shrugged. "I haven't spoken to Becky since the office Christmas party—and then it was only to say hello."

"You and Darren—what do you do for a living?"

"Wealth management."

Pratt took the business card Dewalt offered.

"And what sort of work did Rebecca do?"

"She is…was a teacher. Third grade, I believe." He picked up his coffee, then put it down. "Look, I've got things to do. Hope you don't mind if I cut this short. It hasn't been a good day."

"If I have any more questions," Pratt said, holding up the card, "I know where to find you."

"Sure. Sure. I'd like to help."

Pratt took out his card and slid it across the table. "And if you think of anything, call. Okay?"

Dewalt stuffed the card into the inner pocket of his suit jacket without looking at it.

Pratt watched the man scurry out the far door.

A few minutes later Pratt pushed his tray away and took out his cell phone.

Might as well see what Ellis was up to.

FIVE

"The victim's husband said she ran with her dog every evening, same route," Pratt told Mac at a 9:00 AM meeting the next morning.

Ellis added, "And the spot where it happened is little traveled at that time—especially on a bad night."

Ellis turned his laptop around so Mac could look at the crime-scene photos he'd taken with his cell phone. The young detective took a sip of much-needed coffee while Mac silently went through them. It had been a long night.

Then the questions began.

"This third one. What is it?"

"That's where the murderer parked, waiting for his victim. You can see there where his tires spun a bit as he started after her."

Mac looked up at Ellis. "Has the car been found?"

"Not yet."

Mac nodded. "Keep on top of that." He swung his gaze to Pratt. "Thoughts?"

His best man was famous—or infamous, depending on whom you asked—for playing hunches. The results were often amazing.

Pratt frowned. "A few things are bothering me."

"Follow up on them. I will feel a whole lot happier if we can connect these two victims. A crazy running down random people is *not* something we want to deal with. The public will go nuts."

Pratt stood. "That it?"

"Yes. Keep me up to the minute on this. Clear?"

Both detectives nodded, then left Mac's office.

Walking down the hall, Ellis said, "I don't know about you, but I could kill for some breakfast."

"Good idea. And bring your notes. There are things that need discussing."

Fran's Restaurant near Yonge and College had never smelled so good when they walked in a few minutes later.

SIX

Ellis glanced across the front seat of the car at Pratt, whose eyes were closed, his head back. To anyone else, his partner looked to be asleep. Ellis knew this is what thinking looked like when Pratt did it. He was in awe of how much information the detective could organize in his head.

Pratt's eyes opened. "Both victims are thirty-six. Suggestive. So, were they friends? Had a common friend? We need answers to those questions."

"So that's the tack you want to take with Smith this morning?"

"Yes, but gently. He didn't sound good on the phone earlier. I'll take the lead. Okay?"

This was the closest Pratt ever got to pulling rank, and Ellis was grateful. Pratt was sensitive to the fact that Ellis needed to establish himself as a detective. More and more, he was letting his less-experienced partner handle interviews. Today wasn't one of those days.

The Smiths lived in one of the nondescript brick houses that lined the streets of North Toronto. Even though it was early spring, pots of pansies decorated the front porch of the house. While the previous day's snow was quickly melting, they looked forlorn.

Darren Smith obviously hadn't slept much—if at all.

"Thank you for seeing us at this difficult time," Pratt said as they shook hands. "My partner, Detective Ellis."

The two detectives sat on the sofa in the tidy living room while Smith took one of two upholstered chairs to the side. Pratt noticed a nearly empty Scotch bottle on the floor next to it.

"We need to ask you more questions," he said as Ellis got out his notebook.

Smith shrugged. "Sure, if it will help."

"We think your wife's death might be linked to a similar one that happened recently. Did your wife ever mention someone named Bruce Moore?"

Smith looked blank.

"Doesn't ring a bell."

"Think back to the past few days. Anything odd happen? Did Rebecca seem normal?"

"Provincial tests are coming up. That always makes her tense."

"Nothing else?"

He thought for a moment.

"She was in a good mood on Sunday evening until she checked her email."

"Did you ask about that?"

"She said a parent had an issue, and she'd have to deal with it."

"Do you think that was true?"

"Rebecca wasn't in the habit of lying to me."

"So after the email how did she seem?"

"Distant. We were watching a movie she'd picked, but she paid no attention to it."

"Yesterday morning?"

"Still distant."

Ellis looked up from his note taking. "And it came in on her computer, not her cell phone?"

"She was in the kitchen checking her email before the movie started. I heard her mumble a profanity. She came out a moment later, and, as I said, she seemed distant, like she was worried. That's when I asked her why."

Pratt shifted at his end of the sofa. "We need to look on her computer."

"Do you have to?"

"It may very well help."

"I don't know…"

Ellis said, "We could get a search warrant for it."

"But we don't want to do that," Pratt added. "Will you help us?"

"I should speak to a lawyer first."

"That is, of course, your right. But it will slow our investigation." He leaned forward. "Look. We want to nail the person who did this to your wife. There may be a clue in her emails. Will you help us?"

Darren Smith's sigh was heavy. "If you put it that way…"

SEVEN

Later, Pratt and Ellis sat at their desks, studying preliminary information from the crime-scene techs.

"Certainly gets here a lot faster than it used to," Pratt said, leaning over Ellis's shoulder to look at his laptop's screen. The image on it was a distance shot taking in the entire crime scene. "Our murderer picked a good spot. With that three-meter fence along the sidewalk, there was no way he could miss."

"And I'm betting the vehicle used was stolen. Even if we find a witness, we won't know much more."

Pratt returned to his desk. "Well, if it *is* some random crazy, we're in trouble."

Ellis looked over the screen at Pratt. "You don't believe that."

"No. But if we can't connect the victims, we have to consider it."

Ellis knew what he wanted to do. But, being the junior partner, he felt it wasn't his place to speak first. Pratt stared into the distance for a few minutes.

"Okay, David. Go over everything we've got from the two rundowns. There's got to be something that connects them. Find it. Anything you question, let me know. But first, look at Rebecca Smith's computer. We need to know what's on it."

Which was exactly what Ellis would have suggested.

"I'm burning a mirror copy of her hard drive." Ellis looked at the two computers taking up space on a neighboring detective's desk. "It should be done in twenty minutes, and then I'll send hers back to her husband."

"Call me immediately if you find anything useful."

"And what are you going to be doing?"

"That friend of the family I mentioned who was at the hospital last night? He warrants another chat. Something feels wrong about him being there."

= = =

Computers were something Ellis just understood. At one time, he'd thought being in IT would be his career. Then, in his first year of university, something happened that turned his whole life upside down. Suddenly policing was the only thing he could see himself doing.

But he still enjoyed "messing with computers," as his wife called it, and he was amazingly adept at it. Locked or encrypted files laid open their contents for him easily.

Secrets cleverly hidden were never an issue for long.

Rebecca Smith had little to hide, but even so, the young detective didn't like looking. Going through someone's computer made him feel like a peeping tom.

That weekend email Smith had mentioned was his quarry. It wasn't in her inbox. It wasn't in her trash. He did a global search of her files and came up dry.

She'd obviously deleted it. Interesting—considering how many old emails she had.

It would still be on her computer, of course. Deleted files were never actually deleted. Their locations were just "lost" by the computer. He'd have to wait days for one of the computer techs to dig it off her hard drive byte by byte.

But Ellis had an ace up his sleeve. There might well be a copy left out in plain sight—in Rebecca's webmail. If she was like most people, her emails stayed in her webmail inbox even if she checked them on her computer, and Ellis might find them there.

It didn't take him long.

The email he was looking for had the subject line *it's happened. we need to talk n/t.*

EIGHT

Based on experience, Pratt thought it best to show up at Dewalt's workplace unannounced. Something about the man seemed greasy. It was best to just spring out at people like this unawares, and see what the surprise factor could shake loose.

Mayfield & Young Wealth Management had offices on the twelfth floor of Commerce Court. Even the reception area spoke of money—and lots of it. There were two receptionists, one to answer the phone, the other busy on a computer.

Pratt approached the one answering phones.

"I'd like to see Curt Dewalt."

"Do you have an appointment?"

Pratt pulled out his ID. The girl looked at it, eyes big, then promptly picked up the phone.

She didn't call Dewalt.

A few minutes later a tall gray-haired man came through the inner office door. His smile looked glued on as he approached with his hand out.

"Detective Pratt?"

"Detective Sergeant Pratt, yes. I'm here to speak with Curt Dewalt."

"About what?"

"I'm afraid I can't tell you that."

"This is very awkward. You can't see him."

"Why not?"

"He's not here at the moment."

Pratt, temper short from too little sleep, was losing patience.

"Can you tell me where he is?"

"Ah, he didn't show up for work this morning."

Shit, Pratt thought, but said aloud, "Is there someplace we could talk?"

Once behind the man's closed office door, Pratt bluntly asked him who he was.

"Harris Mayfield, one of the senior partners. You'll have to excuse me today, but the wife of one of our associates tragically died last night in a traffic accident. Is that what this is about?"

Pratt didn't want to give anything away.

"What can you tell me about Curt Dewalt?"

"Well, he's been with us for five years. His results have been good."

"Any work-related issues?"

"He considers himself a Don Juan. Two secretaries have complained about his attentions. We had to discipline him as a result. He's kept a low profile since then, but I doubt if he's, ah, mended his ways."

"And you intend to do nothing?"

"If there are no further complaints, no."

"And his absence today—has this sort of thing happened before?"

"To the best of my knowledge, no."

"And there was no phone call? No email?"

"Frankly, we're concerned. Now you're here. I must know—is Dewalt in any trouble?"

"I just wish to speak to him." Pratt reached into his jacket pocket. "My card. If you hear from him, please let me know. Now, I'd like his home address, if you'd be so kind."

Pratt was back on the street again five minutes later. He was in the act of pulling out his cell phone when it rang.

"Pratt?" came David Ellis's voice. "I've got our email from Rebecca Smith's computer. Where are you?"

"Corner of King and Bay. Come down and pick me up. We're going to Curt Dewalt's condo."

There was silence on the line. "How did you know?" Ellis finally asked.

"Know what?"

"That the email was from Dewalt."

= = =

Dewalt lived in one of the condo towers near the mouth of the Humber River, west of downtown. The only reason a patrol car wasn't dispatched to bring him in was that Pratt wanted to see the sort of place he lived in. It could tell him a lot.

A young man was seated at the building's front desk.

Pratt and Ellis flashed their IDs. The kid went from cocky to solemn in a heartbeat.

Pratt said, "Which apartment is Curt Dewalt's?"

He keyed something into the computer in front of him. "He's in 1807. Is he in trouble?"

"Why do you ask?"

"'Cause you're cops."

"We just want to talk to him," Ellis said.

"He's not here."

"How do you know?"

"He left in a taxi early this morning. He hasn't returned."

"He didn't take his car?"

"Dewalt doesn't have one. Says he hates cars."

Both detectives looked at each other.

The kid went on. "Seems sort of stupid to live way out here when he doesn't drive. The guy must spend a fortune on cabs. Hardly ever takes transit, far as I know."

"Was he carrying anything? A suitcase maybe?"

"No. But he did have a large shopping bag."

Ellis leaned over the desk and handed the kid his card.

"Your name?"

"Um, Fedorsen. Jon Fedorsen."

"Well, Jon Fedorsen. When Dewalt shows his face, how 'bout you give us a call?"

"Sure. I can do that. Want me to tell the evening guy?"

"We'd appreciate that."

= = =

Back in the car, Ellis turned to Pratt.

"What do you make of that? First sign of trouble, and our suspect bolts."

"I don't think he's a suspect."

"How so?" Ellis asked as he eased out into the traffic.

"I *had* thought he might have tagged along to the hospital last night because the job hadn't been completed on Rebecca Smith. As soon as she died, he split. Not the mark of a true friend. He seems to have come back home, gathered some things and taken off. Why? If he was our murderer, what did he have to fear now that she is dead? Running now makes him look bad." Pratt shook his head. "He's scared. And he definitely knows what's going on."

Ellis was silent as he drove east on Lakeshore Boulevard.

Even though he'd had a big breakfast, it was now after four, and Pratt's stomach was rumbling.

"How about some fish and chips? I know a good place up on Burnhamthorpe. On me."

Ellis frowned. "Something tells me I ought to be home and hungry at dinnertime tonight. Jen is still really angry with me. Last night did *not* go down well with her."

"Could I treat you both to dinner?"

"I think tonight will be about staying home with her. As a matter of fact..."

Ellis slipped into a driveway and made two calls. The first one was to his wife, telling her he'd handle dinner. The second

was to preorder said dinner from their
favorite sushi restaurant.

Pratt didn't get why raw fish was a suit-
able dinner, but then, he'd been brought up
on things like fish and chips.

"Could I at least buy you a bottle of
wine?" he asked.

Ellis smiled. "That would be very kind.
Thanks, boss."

"Don't call me that," Pratt growled, but
he was smiling. "And there won't be any
calls. I'll handle anything that comes up
tonight."

= = =

Though they knocked off early, both men
spent a good part of their evenings moving
the investigation forward.

Pratt spent his on the Internet, reading
the coverage their case was getting. The
media had it all wrong, of course. But he
noted Mac being quoted as saying that it

wasn't about "some random crazy" and "we'll get to the bottom of it. Have no fear."

The detective wished his boss had spoken with him first.

Ellis waited until his wife's breathing showed she was asleep before slipping out of bed. In the room they hoped would someday become a nursery, he sat at his computer and began a search. He'd had an interesting idea and wanted to try it out.

His night was again a very late one.

NINE

Pratt was on the phone to Ellis at eight the next morning.

"We're driving out to Burlington to talk to the first victim's wife again."

Ellis sounded like he had a mouthful of cereal when he answered, "I thought that might be on our docket today."

"I want to see if our second victim's name or Dewalt's shake anything loose. I've had cases break wide open on a lot less."

"Put your coffee down, if you're holding it," Ellis said. "I've got something to tell you."

"It's down."

"I had an idea during dinner last night. I didn't say anything to Jen. She's just started to thaw over our ruined date night."

"Very wise."

"Anyway, after she'd fallen asleep I went online to try out my theory."

"And?"

Ellis took a deep breath. "I don't think there are two victims. There are three."

"Continue."

"Six weeks ago in Ottawa, another person was run down in what's nearly a carbon copy of our crimes—caught unawares, a fatal hit-and-run, no witnesses, car used was stolen. Too close for a coincidence, eh?"

"Any other things the same?"

"Only the age. The victim was thirty-six, female, never married. She worked for the government. I got in touch with the Ottawa police and asked for someone connected with the case to call us. So we have another victim's name, and we should use it this morning."

"Did you check for any other hit-and-runs?"

"Nothing so far, but Canada's a big country."

= = =

Ellis picked up his partner at the Kipling subway station. Pratt tossed a copy of *Metro*, the free transit newspaper, between them on the seat.

"Got your picture in the paper, young feller."

It was a photo of Ellis at the accident scene, talking to a crime-scene tech. The caption said something about the poor weather being a factor in the accident—which certainly wasn't the case. But often it helped to have the media go off in wrong directions.

The drive to Burlington took over an hour due to the traffic. Using the GPS on Ellis's phone, Pratt actually got them to the late Bruce Moore's home without a single error. Ellis didn't tell his partner he could have done it without the help.

Susan Moore still looked drawn and sad when she opened her front door. Hovering in the background were her dead husband's parents.

"The brave Toronto detectives," she said. "Do you finally have word about Bruce's death? Have you caught the person who murdered my husband?"

"I'm sorry about the slow pace of our investigation," Pratt answered evenly. "May we come in? There have been developments."

"That hit-and-run the other night?" asked Bruce Moore Senior, looking pleased with himself.

Ellis didn't like him. The gray-haired man obviously considered himself the smartest man in any room.

"May we come in, Mrs. Moore?" Pratt repeated.

Once seated in the living room, the elder Moore asked, "Well?"

His wife finally spoke up. "Bruce, Susan, we should offer our guests coffee or tea."

Both detectives accepted, and she bustled from the room.

"As you guessed," Pratt began, "this is about that hit-and-run Monday night. It has many things in common with Bruce's death. We feel there may well be a connection."

Ellis, eager to get on with it, added, "Do the names Rebecca Smith, Sara Penrose or Curt Dewalt mean anything to you?"

Susan Moore immediately said, "The first person was the one killed the other night." She considered a moment longer. "The others mean nothing to me."

"Think back. They may have been old friends of your husband."

She turned to her father-in-law. "Dad?"

Moore shook his head. "Never heard of any of those people. But if only two have been run down, my son and the Smith woman, who are the other two?"

Ellis was about to answer, but Pratt got in first.

"I'd rather not say at this point. We believe there is a connection between all these people."

"And that's all you're going on? Seems a pretty slender hope."

"I've been successful with less."

"So you say. I must admit that I'm very disappointed by the lack of progress you boys have made. It has been three weeks."

"We're doing our best."

"You're lucky I'm not your boss."

His wife's returning with a tray diffused the situation. Ellis could tell his partner was steaming more than the pot of coffee.

Pratt drew them into a conversation about their son and the family. He asked the mother if the three names rang a bell.

"My son had a girlfriend named Sarah— or something like it—the summer after he was a senior in high school. We summered in Muskoka, you know, before we sold the cottage. He met her up there."

"And where was that?"

"Near Port Carling. Her name wasn't Penrose though."

Pratt turned to Ellis, who said, "Penrose wasn't married."

"We need to check that," Pratt told him before turning back to the older woman. "You wouldn't remember this girl's last name, would you?"

"It was uncommon. Eastern European, I think—at least, it sounded like that."

"Well, if you recall it, can you please let us know? It could be very important."

Less than ten minutes later, the two detectives were on their way back to Toronto.

"The old woman may have given us our first connection," Pratt said, then added, "However tenuous."

"There are a lot of girls named Sara."

"I meant Muskoka. We need to do a complete workup on our four people's pasts. Where they went to school, where they grew up, went to university—the works. Hopefully, the Ottawa police have already done some digging of their own."

"It's going to take time."

"Then we'd better get busy."

TEN

The two detectives spent the rest of the afternoon doing a workup on the three victims and Dewalt. Pratt focused most on Dewalt.

A good three hours into their research, Ellis pushed his chair back and looked at Pratt, whose desk faced his.

"The Penrose woman grew up in Montreal. The detective in Ottawa leading the investigation into her murder is booked off for a week. I spoke to someone who's going to send us everything they have on her. There doesn't seem to be a connection with Muskoka though—but why would they ask about something like that? So it's no wonder they don't have anything. Where do you stand with Dewalt?"

"I spoke to Darren Smith again. Curt grew up in Calgary. I got the feeling it didn't surprise him to hear Dewalt had disappeared. A few other things came out. Rebecca Smith had a relationship with Dewalt during their time at university. She told her husband she couldn't even explain why it had happened, that she'd never really liked Dewalt. It lasted only a month and then she switched schools. That's sort of interesting. When he showed up in Toronto, she hadn't been happy but got her husband to help out an old friend."

"Are you going to dig deeper on Dewalt?"

"I'm already doing that. I called a previous employer. Maybe that will shake something loose. By the way, he still hasn't shown up at his condo as far as the front desk knows." Pratt's chair creaked loudly as he leaned back.

"One positive thing though—Rebecca Smith grew up in Port Carling, maiden name Collins. Dad was a big wheel in the area."

"We should talk to her parents."

"They winter in Florida. They'll be in town in the next day or so—for their daughter's funeral."

"Brothers? Sisters?"

Pratt shook his head.

They spotted Mac walking toward them, a newspaper in his hand.

"You seen this?" he asked, throwing it across Pratt's desk.

Toronto's only tabloid, the source of much grief to the homicide squad over the years, had done it again. The headline screamed, *A Crazy on the Loose?*

Pratt skimmed the article, then handed it to Ellis before looking up at Mac.

"This is really going to help," he said sarcastically. "How do you want to handle it?"

"Besides wringing the columnist's scrawny neck? I guess we'll have to hold a news conference. Everybody else is going to pick this story up in one way or another. We can't have panic break out."

"It might mean showing some cards I'd rather keep hidden."

Mac sighed loudly. "I know. But it can't be helped. The chief is not happy."

"Are you going to handle it?"

"The chief wants to. That means a briefing from you two."

Ellis looked up from the paper. "We should think about that. How much time do we have?"

"I can give you a half hour before we go upstairs to the chief. His media guy will get the word out to the press—although a lot of the news hawks are already downstairs. We have to be fair to the ones who aren't."

In unison Pratt and Ellis said, "Why?" and then laughed.

Ellis suggested there could be someone out there besides Dewalt who knew something. "Doing this press conference might get us some new information,"

Mac and Pratt glanced at each other. The kid could think.

= = =

In the end, a bit of a white lie was told to the media. They asked the chief to make it sound as if they were closing in on a suspect.

After his statement the chief asked Pratt to field questions, since he was the senior member of the team. No mention was made of the Ottawa victim or Dewalt.

"Really, we want to stress that this isn't a random crazy. We strongly believe these two tragic deaths were simply cold-blooded murder. Why? We don't know, but we're working the case from that angle."

The chief concluded the press conference by again asking for help from the public.

"Our tip line is always open, always confidential. Thank you all for your time."

As he left the room, the chief said to Pratt, Ellis and Mac, "Let's hope that's the end of this stupid speculation. Pratt, I'm counting on you to bring this one home for us. Make it snappy."

"We're trying our hardest, sir."

"Well, don't let me down."

And with that he left the room. Raising his eyebrows, Pratt looked at Ellis and Mac.

= = =

Ellis finished his flowchart. He hoped jotting down bits of the information they'd gathered and putting them on a timeline might help. It was about four feet long and covered with writing.

Pratt came around his desk to study it. "Does this get us any closer to linking the murders?"

Ellis shook his head.

"But it shows us where the questions are. Answer those, and we should get our link. If you look here, we have an age link. They were all thirty-six except for Dewalt, who's a year older. I've also asked Darren Smith if his wife kept any scrapbooks, year-books or boxes of old photos. Same with the Moore family. Maybe they all knew each other as kids."

"We need to search Dewalt's condo." Pratt looked at his watch. "It's nearly seven. You should head home. I'll get the warrant in motion."

As he watched his partner hurry out, Pratt was certain Ellis would be back at it as soon as his wife went to sleep.

ELEVEN

Pratt was jolted out of a deep sleep by his phone. Rolling over, he looked at his bedside clock and groaned. One forty-three. This couldn't be good news.

But it was.

"Sorry to call so late, but I have another connection, and it links all three victims. I don't know if it's exactly what we're looking for, but it's something."

Pratt was instantly awake. "Tell me."

"When I got home, I asked the Ottawa police a question. A detective there emailed an answer around ten. That sent me back to the computer. What's up is this. Sara

Penrose's name was originally Saara, spelled S-a-a-r-a. That's Finnish. Her father's name is Alex Lahti. He lives in Victoria now. I just got off the phone with him. The long and short of it is, his daughter spent her teenage summers in Muskoka at her maternal grandparents' cottage. When she began university, she anglicized her given name and took her mother's maiden name. He doesn't know why, since they had an otherwise good relationship. She wouldn't talk about it with her dad."

"So our Ottawa victim spent summers in Muskoka. Our first Toronto victim's parents had a cottage in that area, and our second T.O. victim was brought up there. I'd say you've gotten us a solid link. Now the question is, does this connect to their deaths? And if so, how?"

"I want to drive up there tomorrow."

"That's what I thought you'd say."

"Can you clear it with Mac? I want to make an early start. The weather's supposed to be dodgy later in the day."

"I'll take care of it." Pratt smiled to himself. "Now get some sleep! You've done good work, David."

"Thanks."

= = =

Pratt knew how things worked after twenty-nine years on the homicide squad.

So he got there early the next morning and dropped into Mac's office as soon as the boss arrived.

"Got some news," he said, taking one of the two hot seats—as the squad referred to them.

Mac put his briefcase down next to the desk and also sat.

"What is it? Good news, I hope."

"Ellis has firmly connected the three victims. I have no idea where it's going to take us though. Victim one, the one in Ottawa, grew up in Montreal. Victim two, the first one here, grew up in Burlington. And victim three grew up in Port Carling. All went to different universities. No relatives in common. They never worked together."

"What's so great about that?"

Pratt carefully explained everything Ellis had uncovered in his digging around and how it connected all three victims.

When he finished, Mac had pursed lips and a look of concentration on his face.

"So if I've got this right," Mac began after a moment, "victim one summered in Muskoka and went out with victim two for a summer. The woman killed the other night—"

"Victim three."

"Right. I suppose we gotta keep all this straight somehow. Victim three was born and raised in Port Carling. That all sounds pretty solid. One of you should head up there to nose around."

"It should be Ellis. I hate winter driving."

"Okay. Tell Ellis to get his butt up to Port Carling. He knows the drill about traveling out of town?"

"I'll remind him."

"Good, because if he doesn't keep receipts and hand everything in right, I'm not going to okay any payback for his out-of-pocket stuff."

"Oh, you know Ellis. I think he reads the regulation books every night before going to bed."

When he got back to his desk, Pratt phoned his partner. "Where are you now?"

"Getting close to Bracebridge to check in with the local OPP detachment before heading over to Port Carling. Snow's sort of bad. Did you talk to Mac?"

"Naturally. He suggested you go to Port Carling and nose around."

RICK BLECHTA

Ellis laughed.

Pratt added, "Just don't report in until you've had enough time to drive up there, okay? Call me first if you come up with anything."

"What are you going to be doing?"

"Searching Dewalt's condo. He's one loose end I am not happy about. I'm also thinking of telling the media that he's a person of interest in this case. Maybe someone will spot him. We've got to find him and learn what he knows. Anyway, good hunting, David."

"You too."

TWELVE

When Ellis had to drive long distances, he just wanted to drive. Keeping one eye on the sky and one eye on the road was not much fun. Parts of Highway 11 had black ice. He had to watch carefully all the time.

Winter still had a firm grip on Cottage Country around Muskoka. There was lots of snow, and the lakes were still completely frozen. Bracebridge hardly looked welcoming, and Port Carling would be less so.

Ellis pulled into the Ontario Provincial Police's parking lot on the edge of town. Inside at the desk, he showed his ID and explained why he was two hundred kilometers north of Toronto. After a brief wait he was shown into an office.

His ID had preceded him. The name on the desk was Inspector Jack LaGrazie, and the man himself was wiry, fit-looking and pushing retirement age.

"So what brings a Toronto homicide detective to the north woods?"

"Homicide," Ellis answered with a smile as LaGrazie tossed back his ID.

Ellis couldn't decide if this was LaGrazie's usual manner or if he was being unfriendly. It probably hadn't been smart to bait him.

"So tell me what you want out of us hicks."

It took Ellis not more than five minutes to lay it out. The inspector listened silently. Then, without a word, he turned to his computer and spent the next five minutes browsing various websites.

Just as he finished, the man Ellis had first spoken to stuck his head in the door and simply nodded. LaGrazie turned back to Ellis.

"Found a nice photo of you at the crime scene the other night. Noticed Toronto had a dusting of snow. Must have created havoc with the traffic." Then he smiled. "You seem legit. How can we help you?"

Ellis relaxed. "We don't know exactly what we're looking for, but our three victims all have connections with this area. I'm up here to test our theory. I need help from someone who's been around for a lot of years. Whatever drew these people together didn't happen recently." Ellis then stopped and smiled too. "At least, that's Pratt's and my theory."

"You work with Merv Pratt? Why didn't you say so? Christ, I haven't thought about him in years. How is the old dog?"

"You know him?"

"I worked in our Toronto detachment for quite a while. Let's just say our paths crossed a few times. He's a good man."

Ellis nodded. Everyone seemed to know his partner.

LaGrazie got back on topic.

"And this all centers on Muskoka? That's a lot of ground to cover, son."

"Port Carling is the place to start. One of the victims was brought up there."

"Name?"

"Rebecca Smith, but her maiden name was Collins."

"The daughter of Bob Collins?"

"Yes. You know him?"

"I know *of* him. Owned a big marina. He still has a cottage near Port Sandfield, I believe. Collins was a big deal around here at one time. Damn! I heard about this on the news the other night. I had no idea it involved someone from the area."

Ellis had his notebook out, taking it all down. "Any other relatives around?"

"Don't know. I only came here five years ago. Management's way of easing me out the door, I think. The fella you need to talk to is old Ray Featherstone. He was a constable up here his entire career. I don't think there's much he wouldn't be able to tell you."

"Where can I find him?"

LaGrazie gave Ellis a phone number and an address in a hamlet named MacTier, then sent him on his way.

= = =

The curving road that took Ellis from Bracebridge to MacTier would have been pleasant to drive in good weather. With snow falling, he had to keep his speed down and watch for hidden ice.

He struck out at Featherstone's house, so Ellis left a note on the door and a message on the answering machine. Then he went in search of lunch in nearby Port Carling.

With still no word from Featherstone, Ellis decided to head out to the marina Rebecca's father used to own.

There was only a skeleton staff on, since it was early April. The only person marginally helpful was the secretary, Amy Winter. She was woman in her early thirties, sort of cute—and she liked to talk.

"Sure, I remember Mr. Collins. He gave me my job, but he sold out, oh, must be fourteen years ago now. He's up here in the summer, but right now he'll be in Florida."

"Do you remember Rebecca at all?"

"She was a few years older than me and far more popular. I mean, her family had money, and some of us up here don't. But she wasn't stuck-up. And pretty? She could get any boy she wanted."

"Do you remember a Sara Penrose? Or she may have been using her dad's name of Lahti at the time."

"Oh, you must mean Saaaaaara," Amy said, then added, "Miss La-di-da. That's what some of us used to call her. She's the kind who gives summer people a bad name. Majorly stuck-up. She and Becky were always together in the summers until the end of high school, and then we never saw her again. When she was around, Becky acted like a completely different person."

Ellis could barely keep a smile off his face.

"Would it surprise you to find out they've both been murdered?"

THIRTEEN

Pratt sat at his desk for a long time after leaving Mac's office. His eyes were half-closed as he leaned back in his chair.

Right then he was trying to slot in what he and Ellis had uncovered and organize the questions that had been answered against the far greater number of questions that hadn't. What Ellis might find in Cottage Country was top of mind at the moment. In some ways, Pratt was sorry he hadn't gone along.

He liked Ellis a lot. The kid had the makings of a first-class detective. He was imaginative but careful. He was also fearless and not beyond making rash decisions. That might well get him into trouble someday. But it was a good trait to have—if kept under control. Pratt knew because he had the same problem.

Pratt needed to make progress of his own that day. That meant finding Dewalt and shaking him down until he spilled what he knew. There was still an outside chance he was their murderer. Pratt didn't think so, but Dewalt certainly knew more than he'd let on. And since he was the only one with information who was still alive, it was critical he be found and interviewed.

= = =

Funeral homes had to be the most depressing places in the world, Pratt mused.

He was standing in the middle of the room where Rebecca Smith lay in her coffin.

The room was jam-packed. The number of children with their parents showed what a popular teacher she'd been. The sound of crying was appalling. A small shrine of photos had been set up opposite the body. Each one showed Rebecca with a huge smile.

Her husband, Darren, seemed to be holding up. Pratt guessed he had to be strong because an older couple next to him were beside themselves with grief. It wasn't hard to guess they were Rebecca's parents. The daughter had looked much like her mother.

Pratt nodded to Darren as he passed and stopped in front of the couple.

"I would like to extend my sincerest condolences for your loss."

Rebecca's dad looked at him closely. "Darren told me when you came in that you're the detective in charge of the case. Have you made any progress? Are you going to catch the animal who ended our daughter's life?"

Pratt sighed. "I'd like to be able to tell you we've caught the person who did it. It's still pretty early."

"Will you *ever* be able to tell us that?"

"We are making progress, I believe." Pratt turned to Darren. "Is there a place I could speak to them alone?"

"There's a small room for the family—in case it gets to be too much. It's just through that door."

Pratt led the older couple out of the room.

According to Ellis, Rebecca's father had owned a marina near Port Carling. His wife had probably been able to stay at home.

"There is no gentle way to start into this," Pratt told them. "We're pretty sure your daughter was murdered by someone from her past. We believe there have been three victims and—"

"Three?" Mr. Collins asked. "The papers said two."

Pratt nodded. "Two in Toronto. But there was also a death in Ottawa six weeks ago. We think it ties in with our case. The similarities are striking."

"And? I assume there's more to your story?"

"The only connection between all three is Muskoka. Do the names Bruce Moore, Curt Dewalt or Saara Lahti ring any bells?"

Collins shook his head immediately. His wife looked up, considering.

"I vaguely remember a Saara Lahti," she finally said. "But no Curt Dewalt. I certainly remember that poor Bruce Moore though. Rebecca saw a lot of him for two summers. He took her sailing on Lake Joseph. She didn't say much, but I think she was sweet on him."

"Mavis, please," her husband said. "You're always saying things like that." He looked at Pratt. "Rebecca was going through her teenage rebellion, thankfully short.

She hardly said two words to us if she could help it."

"You don't remember anything else?" Pratt asked. "It could be very important."

The wife looked inclined to talk but was pulled to her feet by her impatient husband.

"We have to get back," he said. "I don't want Darren shouldering this burden on his own."

Pratt remained in the room for minute or two, considering all he'd just heard and seen.

There might well be more information to be gathered about this.

FOURTEEN

"So I'm thinking it's smarter for me to stay up here overnight," Ellis was saying to his wife. "I'm hoping the guy I need to speak to will turn up in the morning. I checked with Mac, and he's given me the thumbs-up about staying."

"Well, *I* haven't," Jennifer responded in a grumpy voice. "You knew my uncle Marty was only going to be in town one night. Mom was expecting us for dinner."

"You can still go. Anyway, nobody will miss me."

"*I'll* miss you. Damn it, Davy, you're letting me down again! And don't start in with your standard 'it's part of the job' crap. You know you take devotion to duty way beyond what's necessary."

Ellis didn't know what to say. They'd been down this road too many times lately. He'd talked to Pratt about it a little, this friction with Jen. That's when he'd found out his partner's wife had walked out on him for pretty much the same thing.

It was all so depressing. He loved Jen truly, madly, deeply, as they always joked. Now it felt as if she was slipping away. He'd thought she understood what his job involved. He was only trying to get ahead so they'd have a better life—a better life for their eventual family.

Jen was still just as angry when the call ended. Well, he had the long trip back in the morning to think of some way to make it up to her.

His afternoon had been frustrating. Unable to find Featherstone, he'd visited

various businesses in Port Carling and the surrounding area. Luckily, he'd brought along photos of Dewalt and the three rundown victims.

The photos hadn't been of much help. People's looks change a lot between their teens and their midthirties. For two of the victims, some people remembered the names, a few the faces, but no one remembered Curt Dewalt at all. And nobody gave Ellis anything usable.

Everyone remembered Becky Collins, of course. She seemed to have been well liked. As the afternoon went on, word was traveling ahead of him that she'd been murdered. He'd hoped that wouldn't happen.

He did find one person who remembered Bruce Moore. Surprising, since the Moores were cottagers, and those people tended to hang around only with their own kind.

The person who'd known Moore looked to be in his late sixties and worked in Port Carling's supermarket. He'd called Moore a city punk, spitting it out like a curse.

"Why do you say that?" Ellis had asked.

"Didn't like the company he kept."

Ellis had pressed, but the man refused to say more.

Other than that, Ellis couldn't dig up anything new.

He drove back to Ray Featherstone's house but found it dark and deserted. In a bit of luck, a neighbor drove up.

"Can I help you?"

Ellis showed the man his ID and said he wanted to talk to Featherstone about an old case. "The OPP detachment in Bracebridge said Ray was the person to talk to."

The man in the car looked suspicious. "Ray ain't around."

Ellis carefully kept his face blank. "I know that."

"He's visiting his daughter in Kingston. Might be back next week though."

"I need to talk to him ASAP. Know the daughter's name?"

"It's Mary."

"Last name?"

"Don't know. She's married now."

"Thanks for the information."

As Ellis walked back to his car, the man stuck his head out the window and shouted.

"I'm going to have my eye on Ray's place. Don't try anything!"

Ellis had gotten a room in a Bracebridge motel for the night. He went back there, turned on the TV and stewed.

He'd pissed off his wife for absolutely no reason. It had been a complete waste of time to stay overnight.

= = =

Ellis never slept well when Jen wasn't cuddled beside him. That night was no exception. He tossed and turned and watched the hours creep by on the cheap motel-room clock.

The smell was what woke him, made him instantly aware. Stabbing at the switch for the bedside light, his eyes shot around the room. Small wisps of smoke were curling in under the door, and they were gathering strength.

Jumping from the bed, he moved to the door and felt it with his hand. Hot. Very hot. He knew better than to open it.

The window in the bathroom was high up and too small. Ellis checked it just to make sure. He might be able to manage it, but he might also get stuck. Heaven only knew what was beneath the window on the outside.

Back in the main room, the only option was obvious—the window next to the front door. He looked around the edge of the curtain. Flames were beneath that too.

Wearing only boxers, Ellis sat on the bed and took the time to slip on his boots. No way would he go out that window in bare feet, with glass all over the place.

"This is not going to be fun," he mumbled to himself.

The paint on the door was beginning to blister at the bottom. There was no sound of help arriving outside.

His eyes were smarting as he picked up a wooden chair next the room's dresser, hefting it for weight. He'd only have one shot at this.

Grabbing the curtain in both hands, he yanked everything right off the wall. The rod clipped his head as it flew by. Flames were halfway up the window. Whoever had lit him up had done the job well.

The window had a thick metal frame with small panes that could be slid open at the bottom and two large panes above. He'd have to go out the upper part, since he doubted he could smash out the center strip. Best to smash out the glass, then use the chair to clear the shards.

Ellis took a deep breath and picked up the chair again.

"Now or never, Davy boy."

Backing up a few steps, he charged the window with the chair legs out. Even though he didn't hit the frame, it jarred him. But the glass shattered, and he quickly cleared the frame of shards. The flames roared up, underneath the door as well as outside the window.

Then he found himself outside on the asphalt, not sure how he got there. By that time people had appeared, and he was aware of distant sirens.

FIFTEEN

"Ellis, you look like death warmed over," Mac observed. "Go home and rest. We can deal with this later."

"I'd prefer to do it now."

Mac did appreciate that Ellis had driven immediately to police headquarters from Bracebridge after the OPP told him he could leave. His left hand was bandaged where it had been cut. His eyebrows were singed off, and he had first-degree burns on his arm—and elsewhere. Still, it could have been a lot worse.

"I'm sure you're going to be hearing from Jack LaGrazie, if you haven't already," Ellis told Pratt.

"You met him? Where is that old so-and-so now? Bracebridge?"

"He's in charge of the detachment."

"A high flyer? Who would have guessed? I can't wait to hear from him."

Ellis had already told Mac and Pratt his story and now wanted to discuss next steps. *Then* he'd go home to get some sleep—and try to explain to Jen what had happened.

"Obviously, I stirred up something," Ellis began.

"Did you run into anybody up there you suspect?" Mac asked.

Ellis thought for a moment. "Not really."

"It shows we've touched a nerve," Pratt said, "but it also tells us something else really important."

Mac raised his eyebrows. "What's that?"

"Our boy isn't through yet."

"So now you think our suspect is male? Based on what?"

"Using a car to snuff out people's lives could be a female thing as well as male, but I can't see a female setting a fire like this. That's a male thing to do."

"And as for our boy not being through yet?"

"If this was over, why try to kill a cop? That's *really* asking for it. If he were done, why not just disappear?"

Ellis sat up and said, "So what do we do about it?"

"Two things. Keep digging in Muskoka. *Something* had to set all this in motion. Since our victims left the area around the time they went to university—and, interestingly, never really went back—then it must have happened at the end of high school. We have them all in this common location at that point in time. That's where we'll find our answer.

"Second, we need to find Curt Dewalt. Obviously, he's been spooked by this and has gone into hiding. He can also give us our answers—as long as he's alive."

"Another news conference?" Mac suggested.

Pratt nodded. "Let's call Dewalt a person of interest and ask again for anyone with information to step forward."

Mac thought for a moment. "We have to go national on this. Who's to say the next victim is anywhere near Toronto?"

Ellis added, "Who's to say Dewalt is anywhere near Toronto?"

"He's still in the country," Pratt said. "I checked with Border Services yesterday. He's still in the country as far as they know. And now they'll be watching for him."

"I'll arrange the news conference, Pratt," Mac said as he stood. "I want you to take the lead on this. The chief might want in, but I think you need to do the talking." He looked at Ellis. "And you, get your ass home. I don't want to see you here before tomorrow at the earliest. Got that?"

Meeting over, Ellis went to his desk to pick up his belongings, which were piled into a plastic garbage bag LaGrazie had given him. He hadn't lost much, because the fire had been put out quickly, but everything was wet and smelled of smoke. A flannel shirt and jeans had been loaned to him by a constable who was his size.

He was bone-tired when he stuck his key in his apartment door. He wanted to do some work to move the case forward. *How do you do that when you can barely think?*

Jen rushed forward when he stepped in. She buried her face in his chest.

"Why are you here?" he asked. "I thought you were working."

"Pratt called me. At least someone communicates. Why didn't you tell me what happened, you big oaf? I'm only your damned wife!"

Ellis kissed the top of her head. "I didn't want you to worry, Jen. I'm all right. I got out, no problem."

She stepped back and looked him over.

"Hands bandaged, limping and no frigging eyebrows left. You call that *no problem?*" But her expression was softer than her words. "And that garbage bag stinks of smoke." Finally she smiled. "Come to think of it, you do too. Give me the bag and get in the shower. Now, mister!"

"Let me get my cell phone and laptop out first. I don't need those washed."

"If you think you're doing any more work today, forget it."

= = =

"I'm sorry to be calling so late, but—"

"David, why are you whispering?" Pratt asked.

"I don't want Jen to know I got out of bed to call you."

Pratt laughed. "I won't tell. Promise. What can I do for you?"

"While Jen was making dinner, I spent a bit of time on the computer. I was looking for anything that might have happened around Port Carling in the summer after those kids finished high school. It took a bit of digging and one phone call, but I may have something."

"The death of Marni Cunningham?"

Ellis took the phone away from his ear, staring at it in shock.

"How did you know?" he asked.

"Our press conference this afternoon shook something loose. The tip line got a call from a pay phone at Union Station. Now get back to bed. I want you to be of some use tomorrow."

"How do you expect me to go to sleep after that?"

"Then go in and cuddle against that wife of yours—before she discovers you snuck out of bed to call me."

Had his wife been awake, Jen would have seen the surprised expression on Ellis's face when he did as he'd been told.

Pratt had never made such a personal remark before.

SIXTEEN

"**Y**our press conference," the female voice began, sounding shaky. "This is about an accident eighteen years ago near Port Carling. Someone was struck and killed. A boy went to jail. He didn't do it."

Pratt pressed the spacebar on his laptop to stop the recording.

"That's all we got before she hung up," he told Ellis.

"I got up early this morning and printed out the few newspaper reports I found online." Ellis handed Pratt several pieces of paper. "I also got in touch with the OPP in Bracebridge. We need to request the trial transcripts and any records of the investigation."

Pratt slid a sheet of paper covered with notes over to his partner.

"Electronic records aren't complete yet for this far back, but I've made some notes. If what this woman tipped us to is legit, we're looking at an old-fashioned case of revenge."

Ellis nodded. "As for our perp, he's Daniel Johnson. Here's what the OPP could give me. No prior record before being charged with vehicular homicide eighteen years ago. The trial was quick. He was in prison sixteen months later. That's all I've got so far."

"I got a bit more. Johnson was paroled a year ago and promptly disappeared from a halfway-house program."

"Definitely sounds like he could be our man."

"Finding him will be difficult. I wonder if he was in Muskoka and set the fire that singed off your eyebrows so nicely."

"Don't you think that would have been too dangerous for him? I mean, he's known around the area, isn't he?"

"I called LaGrazie when the tip came in, and he's looking into that. He mentioned some old cop named Featherstone. Isn't that the guy you were hoping to talk to?"

Ellis nodded and answered, "Yeah, the one who's never at home."

"LaGrazie said he'd try to get in touch with Featherstone for us and have him call." Pratt leaned back and raised his eyebrows. "And Featherstone was the arresting officer in the Cunningham death."

"You think that's why someone tried to light me up at the motel?"

It was Pratt's turn to nod. "Makes sense, doesn't it? You'd been all around Port Carling asking questions that day. Word gets around quickly in small towns. Did you ask about Featherstone?"

"I may have. My memory is a little fuzzy. I'll check my notes."

"Do that."

The two detectives worked their new leads separately for the rest of the morning, sharing information as it came in. The trial of the Johnson boy had been big news in Muskoka, but hardly registered in the Toronto or national media. Ellis had to really dig for information and photos. No mention was made of anyone else being involved, although he did find one article that reported Johnson claimed he was not alone in the car at the time of the accident.

Shortly after noon, two things happened. Records about Johnson's time in jail arrived, and Mac stuck his head out the door of his office, shouting for Pratt and Ellis.

Both men got up from their desks, eyebrows raised.

"Good news or bad?" Ellis asked.

"Hard to tell. He didn't sound angry."

"Sit down, boys," Mac said with a smile when they arrived at his door. "Tell me where you're at."

Fifteen minutes later their boss had heard the condensed version of where Pratt and Ellis had gotten to.

His smile only broadened.

"Now, I've got a little present for you two," Mac said, leaning back in his chair. "I just got off the phone with my RCMP counterpart in BC. He heard about our murders. Guess what? Based on the details, he's dealing with one of his own. A male victim, one Thomas Lamport, same age as our victims, hit while jogging near his cabin on Vancouver Island. No suspects, few clues, stolen car found later in Victoria. They're literally begging for our help. The dead man was a major real-estate developer, and they've made almost no progress on the case. They were working the angle that it might have something to do with a deal gone bad. He'd had a few of those in the past few years." Mac scribbled a name and number on a sticky note, handing it to Pratt. "I told him you'd be in touch ASAP." As the two detectives got up to leave, he added, "And by the way, great work, you two. Isn't that worth losing your eyebrows over, Ellis?"

SEVENTEEN

"LaGrazie said you were looking for me," a scratchy voice said over the phone.

Ellis, back at his desk, had just pulled out the sandwich Jen had made for him that morning.

"Ray Featherstone?" he asked.

"That's me. You the guy who was prowling 'round my house two days ago?"

"I came to your house looking for you, if that's what you mean."

"Sorry. No offense intended. That's just the word my neighbor Dan used."

Featherstone coughed rawly. It didn't sound good.

"I have a few questions for you," Ellis said.

"So I gather. LaGrazie said it had something to do with Bob Collins's kid, Becky."

Ellis resealed his sandwich inside the plastic box. He'd gladly forgo his meal to speak to Featherstone.

It took twenty minutes to run down what he and Pratt knew and why they believed the nexus of events led back to Featherstone's old beat.

"Cunningham. Yeah, I remember that one. Nasty business. She was walking along the side of Peninsula Road, north of Port Sandfield. Not that dark a night, and she had on light-colored clothes. Older woman. If memory serves, fifty-five or thereabouts. Some punk in a stolen car, driving too fast, didn't see her in time. He hit the brakes and even managed to stop quickly—with his frigging left front tire right in the middle of the Cunningham woman's abdomen.

He backed off her, and I happened along maybe five, ten minutes later. Caught him red-handed, crouched right next to her."

"And that was Daniel Johnson."

"Correct."

"He had no priors. What can you tell me about him?"

"His family owned a gas station in Port Carling. They also still did repairs. Imagine that? Danny was a bit of a wild kid, but smart and clever. Never got caught for anything. Natural ringleader, if you know what I mean. His dad finally lowered the hammer, and Danny seemed to calm down toward the end of high school. Even got a scholarship to university.

"Then he stole a car and threw himself and his family into the toilet. They lost the gas station paying for his defense. There was no way even the best lawyer in the country could have gotten him off. Don't you have the court records?"

"We just got tipped to this. You know how slow these things are."

Featherstone laughed, then said, "Don't I ever. That's why I was happy to be a backwoods cop my whole career. Less paperwork BS."

Seeing the way Featherstone felt, Ellis phrased his next question carefully.

"Did you ever suspect there might have been something else going on, other people involved?"

"Oh, you mean Danny boy saying there were other kids in the car and he wasn't the one driving? Didn't happen. Just plain didn't happen. Don't you believe it for an instant."

"We got a tip yesterday that led us to the Cunningham death, and it came from a woman who also said Johnson didn't do it. The only connection we've got between all four murdered people is Muskoka. Johnson was paroled last year and promptly disappeared. The murders began several months later, starting in British Columbia. Everything points to him being our man. But why would he murder these people? And do it with a car each time? Any thoughts?"

Featherstone was silent for a few beats. "You can believe what you want, but I was there, and I know. Of course the investigation went down that rabbit hole of Johnson's—and found zilch."

Featherstone cut off the interview at that point, saying he had places to go.

Ellis hung up, thinking to himself, You better hope the killer doesn't come after you next, Featherstone.

He looked up to see Pratt returning with a Reuben sandwich and coffee, his favorite lunch. Sitting down at his desk, Pratt opened the coffee and took a sip.

"Sorry I was gone so long. Did I miss anything?"

EIGHTEEN

The two detectives spent the better part of the afternoon following up leads. After the press conference the previous day, quite a few had come in rapidly. They always did when Pratt spoke to the media. Mac's theory was that he always looked so sad, people wanted to help. Pratt thought it was because he came across as thoughtful and open. Ellis wisely stayed out of it.

The leads had been vetted by other staff, who passed the ones that might be worthwhile over to Pratt and Ellis. Looking at these slowed down the more important work of digging into Daniel Johnson's background, but Pratt insisted that they do this themselves. After all, he and Ellis had the most complete knowledge of the case.

In between, Pratt got in two calls to contacts in Corrections Canada. Late in the day, one of them bore fruit.

"For you," Ellis said as he held out the phone. "Someone named Jones."

Pratt leaned forward and took the receiver. "Pratt. Talk to me, Alex…Yeah?… And he'll speak to me?…You're sure?…This is great. I owe you, buddy…Yeah, I know you will…Okay, I'll take it from here."

He had a broad smile as he handed back the phone.

"What was that about?" Ellis asked.

"An old friend did a bit of spade work for us."

"And?"

"Johnson did his time at Collins Bay Institution. Alex is the assistant warden. I asked him if Johnson was particularly close to anyone, and that call was to say the person Johnson knew best would be willing to talk to me."

"When do you want to go out there?"

"Tomorrow."

"I was planning on heading up to Muskoka again," Ellis said. "For one thing, Johnson's father still lives up there. I also want to ask around the area about Featherstone, see if he's the sort of cop who might be bought off."

"You'll need to be discreet about that one."

"Hey! It's me. Discretion is my middle name."

"You and I both know that's not the case." Pratt got up. "Let's go talk to Mac."

= = =

Ellis made a point of getting home on time that day. Returning to Muskoka would not be popular with his wife. To help with that, he disappeared into the bathroom to change the dressings on his hands for smaller ones. The cuts were healing, as were the burns on his face and arms, but it would be weeks before his eyebrows looked normal.

He also made reservations at a small Italian restaurant Jen loved.

She saw through it all immediately.

"So what is it you don't want to tell me, Davy?"

He flashed a sheepish smile. "I have to go to Muskoka again."

"When?" Jen asked, her face troubled.

"Tomorrow morning. First thing."

"Why can't Pratt do it?"

"He's going to Collins Bay, the prison out near Kingston."

"Switch with him."

"I can't. I've been up there. He hasn't. And he's going to interview a potential witness. You know he's better at that stuff than I am."

"I can't believe you're doing this! You could have *died* up there last time."

He reached across the table for her hands. "Please, Jen. It's just something I have to do."

"At least you didn't try to say it was part of your job."

"Scout's honor, I will be careful. As a matter of fact, Mac suggested I get an OPP constable to ride with me as I travel around up there." He tried a smile to see if it would soften her expression. "Two is better than one, like you always say."

"Look, Davy, I knew your job was dangerous when I married you. When you became a detective, I was hoping it would be less dangerous than being a plain constable and—"

"But this was the first time anything bad has happened! And yeah, I got a bit singed and cut, but it really wasn't that dangerous. Actually, I should have just stayed in the room and waited for the firemen."

That wasn't quite true, but a tiny lie won't hurt, he thought.

His wife still looked unconvinced.

"Jen, darling, I know how tough it is being a cop's wife. You know I don't take unnecessary chances. But sometimes things happen. I promise I'll have someone with me and will keep both eyes open for danger. I also won't stay overnight. I will be home tomorrow evening—perfectly safe and sound."

Finally, Jennifer Ellis smiled, and while it wasn't her best, her husband relaxed.

For the rest of the evening, police work was out of bounds. They both went to sleep with smiles on their faces. And this time, Ellis didn't get out of bed—though he was sorely tempted.

NINETEEN

Pratt became depressed the moment he stepped inside Collins Bay. Prisons always affected him that way. Now it was a matter of gritting his teeth and getting through the interview.

After signing in and going through ID checks, Pratt was eventually led to one of the small interview rooms. The table and two chairs opposite each other were old and scarred—and fastened to the floor. Drumming his fingers, Pratt waited for nearly thirty minutes.

He was there to see Anthony Whipple. Whipple was a small-time thug who'd

eventually worked his way up to murder—
although he'd claimed it was an accident.

Whipple was nearing fifty. Tall and wiry
with light brown skin and a long face, he
reminded Pratt of a jazz sax player whose
name slipped his mind at the moment.

Sprawling in his chair, Whipple smiled
and asked, "You're Pratt?"

"I am."

"And you want to know about my boy
Danny Johnson."

"I do."

Anthony laughed. "Don't talk much, do
you?"

"That's your job."

The con laughed again and stuck out
his hand. Pratt shook it.

"Pleased to meet you, Pratt. I know a
few boys in here who'd like to see you too."

The detective was through with nice-
ties. If he had Anthony Whipple pegged, he
would respond to directness.

"Just tell me about Johnson," he said coldly. "How well did you know him?"

"First, a bit of business. I got a meeting with the parole board in two months. I need someone to put in a good word for me."

"You know I can't talk about something like that."

"I know everyone says that, but it's done all the time. You willing to help me? Quid pro quo and all that?"

Pratt answered with a shrug.

"Tell me about Johnson," he repeated.

Whipple thought for a moment, then said, "Let's say I was his mentor. Danny was just a wet-behind-the-ears high-school kid when he showed up on our door-step. He would have been eaten alive if it weren't for me."

"So you knew him well."

"I was in the cell next to his for thirteen years."

"And you talked a lot."

"You know cons. It's talk or watch TV. With Danny, talking was good. He's a real smart guy." Whipple shook his head. "He never should have been here."

"Did he tell you that?"

Laughter again echoed in the small room.

"Every *friggin'* day."

Pratt leaned forward. "Look, Whipple, I won't lie. We believe Daniel Johnson is responsible for four deaths over the past several months. We also believe it has something to do with the car accident that got him sent up. Can you tell me anything about what he's up to? There may be more potential victims out there."

"And you remember my request about the parole-board hearing, the one you can't comment on?" The con nodded when Pratt didn't answer. "Danny's killed four people, you say? Well, there should be two more out there, maybe three, depending on what he decided in the end."

"Do you know who they are—the live ones, I mean? We think a man named Curt Dewalt might be on Danny's list."

"He did mention that name."

"But that leaves one or two more. Their names, Whipple, I need their names."

"I'll have to think about that for a bit, if you catch my drift. Last time I spoke to Danny Johnson was almost two years ago. The memory fades."

Pratt's fist crashed down on the table.

"Don't mess around with me, Whipple! Lives are at stake. If I can't get to someone in time because you were playing games, it's going to end badly for you, I swear to God."

"All right, all right. No need to get your panties in a twist. I can see you're a police officer of high principles."

Anthony Whipple began to talk. Pratt took out his notebook and started the small tape recorder he'd brought.

Pratt's memory was excellent, but it made no sense taking chances. No telling what Whipple might do in the future. Pratt knew way better than to trust a convict.

TWENTY

*T*he evening was nearly as hot as the day had
been, not usual for late August in Muskoka.
In the stuffy gas-station office, it was hard for
Danny Johnson to stay awake.

Why did he always get stuck at his family's
gas station on Saturday nights? He knew how
hard his dad and mom worked, but sometimes
it just seemed too unfair. Another boring end to
another boring week of another boring summer.

The nineteen-year-old snorted. What differ-
ence did it make anyway? It wasn't as if he had
friends to hang with—not since Mike had left to
spend the summer planting trees up north. Some
way to pass the last free months of your youth.

The single friend you have goes off, leaving you on your own.

A car pulled into the station, windows down, radio blaring.

"Hey, Johnson!" the kid on the passenger side yelled. "We need gas. Move it!"

The pretty girl beside him added, "And please hurry. We're running really late."

Danny's heart ached. He'd had a crush on Maggie McDonald, a summer visitor, since eighth grade. What he wouldn't give to be the one going out with her tonight.

But he wasn't part of the in-crowd. These were kids whose parents had money and were a big deal in town. Danny's parents owned the local garage.

The car's driver stuck his head out the window. "Didn't you hear the lady, dipstick? We've got to make tracks!"

At the back of the car, Danny unscrewed the gas cap. "Keep your shirt on. I heard you."

Someone in the backseat paid. Walking to the office, Danny heard the car's engine crank uselessly.

"You're going to flood it if you keep doing that," he called out.

A few minutes later Maggie came into the office. "It won't start."

"I sort of noticed."

"Can't you do something? You've lived in this garage all your life. Don't you know anything?"

Maggie's words stung, but he didn't show it.

"I'll look under the hood."

It was clear the car wasn't going anywhere. When Danny told them, they made out like it was his fault. One of the other girls complained about missing "the biggest friggin' party of the summer."

Bruce Moore, whose old man owned property all over Muskoka, loudly complained to the driver about the state of his wheels.

"Hey, man, it's my uncle's car. What can I do? Why don't we use your wheels instead? Oh...that's right. You don't have any."

"Eat shit and die, Curt," Bruce shot back.

Danny didn't really know Curt Dewalt. Midway through July he'd shown up in town and gotten a job at the big restaurant at the far end of town (owned by his uncle). The few times Curt had stopped for gas, he'd come across as a prick.

Sullenly the three boys helped Danny push the car away from the pumps. They continued arguing among themselves as they stomped off.

Since it was late, Danny began to close things down. Back in the office, he was counting the cash in the till when Maggie walked in the door again.

She looked so beautiful. To Danny she was perfection—slender, tall, blond hair in a ponytail. As she removed a stick from a pack of gum and popped it into her mouth, he could barely breathe. He'd never been this close to Maggie before—and they were alone.

"Danny..." she began, her beautiful blue eyes fixed on him. "I have a big favor to ask."

Inside his head, he was screaming, *I'll do anything you want, darling Maggie!* But all that came out of his mouth was a strangled, "What?"

"You know how to hot-wire a car, don't you?"

"Well..."

"C'mon, I heard you talking about it with your friend Mike one day in the supermarket last summer."

Maggie McDonald had heard him talking to his friend? Really?

"Yeah. Sure I can."

She flashed an encouraging smile. *Where was this going?*

"Would you hot-wire a car for me?"

"What?"

Impatience flashed across her face, and then the smile emerged again. "Walk with me and I'll tell you."

Following her out of the office, his attention was focused on her jean-clad rear end. This was like something out of a dream.

"Won't you need some tools?" Maggie asked.

Hardly thinking, Danny went back in, got a few things and locked the door to the office. Side by side, they started down the road toward town.

"Where are your friends?"

Maggie turned her head toward him. "They went on ahead."

"Where?"

"Don't ask so many questions, silly. They're scoping things out." She bumped him with her hip. "Don't worry. It will be okay."

Not wanting her to think he was a wuss, Danny shut his mouth. Maggie chattered on about the party near Rousseau and how awesome it would be. He was surprised. She seemed nervous.

How could Maggie be nervous with him?

It took about fifteen minutes to get to the restaurant where Curt worked. The parking lot was packed. Danny had filled up most of these cars during the summer. What was parked here represented some serious money. Inside the restaurant he could hear a band. The old folks were kicking up their heels tonight.

Maggie stopped, looking around.

"Over here!" someone called softly.

In a dark corner of the lot they found the others, standing around a silver Mercedes.

Danny hung back as Maggie spoke with Curt. Then she came to him.

"This is the car. Can you hot-wire it and not leave any trace?"

"I suppose. Are you sure this is okay?"

"It's Rebecca's parents' car. She left her keys at home. They won't mind." She took his arm and pressed her body against his side. Her perfume filled his nose. "Would you do it, Danny—for me?"

A light near the building caught her eyes, lighting them up.

He gulped.

"Sure."

TWENTY-ONE

Pratt had used a driver that day, since Ellis was up north. He spent the three-hour trip back from Collins Bay staring at his notes and scrolling back through what Anthony Whipple had told him. He'd turned out to be an excellent storyteller.

"Those kids and their parents hung Danny Johnson out to dry. Soon as Curt hit the woman, they all bolted into the bush. Danny backed the car off her body and tried to comfort her as she died. He wasn't even aware they'd cut out on him until the first cop showed up."

"Do you know what happened after-ward?" Pratt had asked.

Whipple rubbed his thumb and first two fingers together, the age-old sign for money.

"Danny told his story to the cops. The kids denied it. Their parents backed up their alibis. All the families were well off. Danny suspects certain cops got paid to not try too hard investigating his side of the story. He was guilty and that was the end of it.

"His family lost everything too, trying to pay for his legal help. The lawyer they got was all but useless. I say it was a lucky day for Danny that Canada doesn't execute people anymore."

Pratt thought for a minute. "You said you weren't surprised Johnson has killed those responsible."

Whipple shook his head. "He spent his entire time inside working it all out.

His life is ruined as he sees it. So they must pay, and he doesn't care what happens to him. I thought it was just talk," he added, covering himself, "but now it seems Danny was dead serious."

"Okay, one last thing. Curt Dewalt has done a bunk. Obviously, he figures Johnson is coming after him, but this sixth person, the last girl, can you tell me anything about her? Did Johnson say where she might be? Time is critical on this."

"I don't think he knew where any of them were. That's probably why it took him some time to start offing them. He needed to have his ducks in a row before he started."

"But the girl's name?"

"It was Maggie. Maggie Mc-something. She was the one who talked him into hot-wiring the car. He insisted on going with them so he could bring it right back, stupid fool. He couldn't decide who he hated most,

Curt Dewalt or Maggie. McDonald! That was her last name."

In many ways, Pratt felt bad for Danny Johnson.

≡ ≡ ≡

Ellis's day in Muskoka wasn't as well spent. Danny Johnson's dad, now almost a hermit in a bush cabin, would hardly speak to him. That was probably because the dad knew something. They could always haul him in for questioning, but that would take time Ellis didn't think they had.

Little progress had been made on the motel fire. Trash had been at hand. Gasoline too. Johnson's dad had an ironclad alibi, and there were no persons of interest on the OPP's radar.

Ellis suggested they look at Ray Featherstone, but LaGrazie's expression when Ellis said that made it clear it would be a hard sell.

The only bit of useful information came from Johnson Senior.

"My son didn't do it. It was those six other kids. They wrecked Danny's life, God rot them! I hope they all fry in hell for what they did."

Then he'd slammed the door in Ellis's face.

The only positive of the day was that Ellis arrived home safe and sound *and* in time to make dinner for his wife.

Trouble was, late that evening Pratt called Ellis.

"We've found Dewalt. Pick me up at home."

"Where was he? Can we talk to him?"

"Scarborough. And no, he's not going to be talking to anybody. This is a bad one, David."

TWENTY-TWO

The murder scene was an abandoned building in the east end. Curt Dewalt had been fastened tightly to the concrete floor by means of bolts and cable ties. He'd died as a result of the front left wheel of a car being lowered onto his abdomen.

Neither Pratt nor Ellis could look at the results for very long. The murder had been slow and cruel as the jack holding up the car was gradually lowered.

Outside the building, both looked at each other, knowing time was running out fast. If Anthony Whipple had told the truth, only one more potential victim remained. So far they'd come up dry on the whereabouts of Maggie McDonald. There were a lot of people with that name across the country—if she even *was* in Canada anymore.

"If we don't get to her first, he's going to complete his revenge and quite likely disappear," Pratt said.

"He's got to suspect we're on to him by now."

"There's the fact he tried to barbecue you."

Ellis shook his head. "I don't think it was Johnson. My money's on his father. He's also an angry man."

"We'll have to put that aside for the moment. Finding the sixth person is our priority."

"How the hell do we accomplish that? If it was Maggie who phoned in the tip, she could have told us then. Obviously, she doesn't want to step forward."

The wind that night was from the north and bitter, so Pratt suggested they sit in Ellis's car. Perhaps it was also a way to get farther away from the horrific crime scene.

"So how do we find our mystery woman before she becomes a victim?"

Pratt thought for a moment.

"Scare the shit out of her," he replied. "Do another news conference first thing tomorrow and convince her she's in grave danger and only we can help. We also name Daniel Johnson as our prime suspect."

Ellis looked at the car's clock. It was after eleven.

"What if he makes his move tonight?"

Pratt slowly shook his head. "If luck is on our side, Maggie McDonald is safely asleep."

"What do we do in the meantime?"

"We write a press release so the media has the word out by the time people get up in the morning. Then we organize our press conference. That means we have a long night ahead of us, David. First of all, we need to share all our information. I learned some interesting things in Collins Bay today, and I believe I have a good handle on exactly what's been going on."

"Then what?"

"Well, we're going to have to convince Mac to drag his sorry butt in to work." Pratt smiled. "He hasn't had to pull an all-nighter in years."

= = =

At nine the next morning, Mac stepped to the podium in the packed Toronto Police Service's media room. He was flanked by the chief and Pratt. His expression was suitably grim.

"Ladies and gentlemen, as you know, we have been investigating the deaths of two people by vehicular homicide over the past several weeks. The number of deaths is now up to five.

"In the past few days the pieces have begun falling together, thanks to the tireless work of the man standing to my left and his partner.

"On the screen to my right is the person we believe responsible for all these killings, Daniel Johnson. He is an ex-convict who was jailed for vehicular homicide when he was nineteen. He was paroled a little over a year ago. We are searching for him now. We consider him very dangerous. Anyone who knows his whereabouts should notify the police. Do *not* approach him."

Mac stopped and asked Pratt to tell the media some of the details. The detective repeated parts of the story Anthony Whipple had told him. Then he went through the list of victims and how each had died, without stinting on details.

Then it was the chief's turn.

"So this is a story of revenge," he told the media, "not the work of a maniac with random victims. It is cold, calculated murder. I'm told Johnson is intelligent and resourceful. You've heard about five dead people. But apparently there is a sixth potential victim. We believe this person phoned in the tip that led us to Johnson. Problem is, she did not tell us her whereabouts. At this point, we are assuming that she is still alive. I am speaking directly to her now.

"Maggie or Margaret McDonald, do not hope that you will avoid your fate at Daniel Johnson's hands by running or trying to hide. He may well know where you are right now. Pick up the phone and call us. We can and will protect you until this very dangerous criminal is captured. Please, do the smart thing. Call."

It was left to Pratt to take the media's shouted questions. It took a long time to satisfy them.

Meanwhile, Ellis was waiting for the call. Minutes ticked by and it didn't come.

TWENTY-THREE

It was after eleven in the morning. Pratt and Ellis looked up as Mac came into his office, actually bringing them coffee. Pratt raised his eyebrows, and his partner grinned. This was different.

Then the chief walked in.

"I've been looking at your reports, boys," he said, "and you've done some mighty fine work. I've had calls from BC and Ottawa, and they're pleased too." He took a sip of the coffee Mac had handed him. "Problem is, what if our potential victim doesn't get in touch? What if Johnson gets to her first? We're going to look bad if you don't pull this one off. Folks are going to say we put a target on her back by telling Johnson how close on his trail we are."

Ellis knew enough to keep his mouth shut. He'd only been in the chief's presence twice. Pratt, the legendary homicide detective, was used to this blame shifting.

"There's not a lot we *can* do. Johnson is smart. We've done the best we can. That's why we laid it on so thick at the news conference and in the press release last night. There's coverage on all the networks, on the media websites and even in one of the morning papers. Now it's a matter of waiting. Who's going to win? Him or us? I'm not a betting man."

The chief got up, took one more swig of his coffee and left. Mac frowned, and Pratt started laughing.

"How come the only time he comes down here," Mac said, "is to piss all over my desk?"

"Relax, Mac," Pratt said. "Pissing is part of the chief's job description."

A shout came from the squad room.

"Hey, Pratt! Your phone's ringing."

Ellis was instantly out of his chair. Pratt and Mac followed at a slower pace.

"Pratt! The caller wants you—and you only," Ellis shouted.

"Male or female?"

"Male. Hurry. He sounds edgy."

Pratt took the receiver. Ellis pressed the speakerphone key.

"Detective Pratt here. Talk to me, please."

"It's my wife," a voice answered almost in a whisper. "I think she's the woman, the one that murderer is after."

"May I speak to her, please? She is in great danger."

"She's not here."

"Where is she?"

"She left for work early, like she always does."

"Where can we find her?"

"Um...that's what the problem is."

"Please tell me where she is. Her life could depend on it."

"Oh god," the man said, sounding as if he was talking to himself. "She will be so angry."

"Angry? Why?"

"She has a secret. She doesn't know I know about it. You see, I read her diary from when she was young. It was forgotten in a box of books."

Mac and Ellis had crowded in along with two other detectives who were in the squad room. Pratt had to jolly this man along until he got what he needed. He kept his voice smooth and level, no hint of the excitement he was feeling.

"What did the diary entry say?"

The man didn't answer immediately. Pratt was afraid he'd hung up.

"There was a car accident. The one you talked about this morning. My wife was in that car. She was sworn to secrecy. It must have been horrible."

"Sir, you need to tell me where she is. There is no other way to help her."

"Oh god…"

"Please tell me."

"It will ruin her. It will ruin us."

"You've gone this far. I know you want to save her life. Just tell me."

The man on the line sighed heavily. "Okay."

TWENTY-FOUR

It all made sense. The sixth person *couldn't* just come out of the shadows. She was a high-flying provincial Crown attorney right there in Toronto. Both Pratt and Mac had worked with her.

Gwen Trudell was a brilliant prosecutor and rumored to be in the running to become a judge very shortly.

And no wonder they'd been unable to find her. Maggie McDonald had left her old name and life far behind.

She didn't have a scheduled court appearance that day, but she was meeting with someone at the provincial courthouse north of Queen Street West on University Avenue.

Unfortunately, that's all her husband knew.

"Gwen doesn't talk about work. I know enough not to bother her. She can be very formidable."

Plans were quickly made. Pratt and Ellis would hightail it to the courthouse, and Mac would call in a SWAT team and get in touch with court security. The sooner Trudell was secured, the better. Then a search could begin for Johnson.

An unmarked car was waiting at the curb with two constables inside when Pratt and Ellis got down to the street.

"You up to speed?" Pratt asked them.

In answer the car took off with a squeal of tires along College, screaming south at University.

"Still no answer on her cell, Pratt," Ellis said as they drove. "It sounds as if it's turned off."

The car's radio crackled.

"Pratt!" Mac said. "Trudell's not in the building. She just left via the back doors. Someone was with her."

"Male or female?"

"Male."

"Shit! Did anyone see where they went?"

"South along the side of Nathan Phillips Square—you know, where the peace garden is."

"Get all cars to hold back. No sirens either. We don't want to spook him. He's got nothing to lose."

"Corner of Queen and University," Pratt told the driver.

"You think he's got a gun?" Ellis asked.

"Either that or a knife. Why else would she leave with him so meekly? I know that woman. She doesn't take any crap."

Ellis had been madly using his thumbs on his cell phone. He passed it forward to the constable not driving.

"That's our perp. Consider him armed and extremely dangerous."

Pratt asked, "And can you get that photo out to every car? I have no idea what is going to go down, but from Nathan Phillips Square, there are dozens of places Johnson could go."

The car screeched to the curb.

"Stay here and watch for them," Pratt told the two constables.

Ellis sprinted to the southwest corner of Nathan Phillips Square. Pratt pulled up just behind him, breathing hard.

"I don't see them," Ellis said. "If they've gotten into the PATH system...that underground warren with all those stores. Christ! There are dozens of exits all over downtown. We're going to need hundreds to search it."

"And evacuate all the people."

"If he hasn't taken her there, then where else?"

"Commandeered a car or taxi?" Pratt offered his phone. "Call it in. And tell them to watch the subway stations connected to the PATH. He could just as easily use a subway train as a car for what he has in mind."

Pratt thought while Ellis spoke to Mac. Johnson was methodical, and this was not just about who died, but *how* they died. He was making them suffer the way the woman they'd killed had suffered.

They weren't in the square or on the street. Where else might they have gone?

Pratt looked around. Where? *Where?*

"Ellis!" he shouted, running forward.

TWENTY-FIVE

Underneath Nathan Phillips Square, the large open area fronting Toronto's iconic city hall, lies a huge four-story parking garage. Pratt knew it had a lot of dark corners and, at this time of day, not that much traffic, especially on the lowest level.

Ellis trotted up.

"Where are we going?"

Pratt told him. "And there are stairway entrances all over the square." He pointed. "See? There—and there—and there. I'll bet he had this all planned."

"You're sure?"

"Of course I'm not sure!" Pratt snapped. "But if I'm right, it won't take him long to do what he needs to do."

"There's the Chestnut Street ramp. That would have been closer."

"Too busy. No, he would have used the stairs."

They ran to the nearest stairway. Pratt turned to Ellis.

"Call it in. We need this whole area secured and men to help search. Follow me when you've done that."

"Where will you be?"

"Lowest level. Fewer people. Who wants to park down there with all these stairs to climb?"

It took Ellis two minutes to get through his call. He started down the narrow concrete staircase. It was gloomy and smelled of urine. At the bottom he pulled his gun and opened the door to the parking level.

Pratt was nowhere in sight.

After a moment's thought Ellis decided to go right down the middle of the level. It would give him his best chance of spotting something. The parked cars would provide decent cover.

The space was large, with not many cars. Ellis ran from one to another, ears straining for any sound, eyes on the move.

Approaching the southeast corner, he heard a sound. A muffled whimper? He peered out from behind an SUV.

In the farthest aisle, he saw a woman in business attire lying on her back. Her hands were behind her, and a cable tie bound her ankles together. He couldn't see her face, but he assumed from the sound he'd heard that she was gagged. Where was Johnson? And where was Pratt?

He took a chance and moved forward one car. He heard an engine start somewhere behind him. The woman put her head up. Ellis was close enough now to see her wide eyes. Johnson was coming, and she knew what he meant to do.

Sticking his head out again, he looked back. No car. It must be in one of the other aisles. Had Johnson seen him sneaking around?

Ellis's mind was working furiously. Should he run to Trudell and drag her out of the way? Should he go find Johnson? Was Johnson armed? The detective was painfully aware of his lack of body armor.

"Jen will be so pissed if I get shot," he mumbled to himself as he looked behind again.

No sign of Johnson. What was he waiting for? His last victim was ready for the kill. Was something wrong? Maybe Pratt had found him.

It was one of those decisions made without conscious thought. One moment Ellis was wondering what to do, and the next he was racing toward the woman.

Her head was up as she struggled frantically. A squeal of tires behind made Ellis turn.

An SUV had just turned the corner and was racing for him. With no time to react, he grabbed Margaret Trudell's feet and dragged her behind a car to his right. If Johnson managed to hit it squarely, they were still in great danger. There was no time to do anything more.

Two shots rang out, then three more, followed by a deafening crunch of metal. Ducked behind the car as he was, Ellis couldn't see what had happened.

He stuck his head up. The SUV had crashed squarely into a pillar about twenty feet away. Curls of steam rose from the crumpled hood.

Gun at the ready, Ellis quickly moved forward to the driver's side. Johnson lay pinned against the seat by an exploded airbag spattered with blood. He was very clearly dead.

Pratt came running up, gun still in his hand.

"Well, that was a close thing."

Ellis said simply, "You saved our lives."

Muffled sounds came from behind the car Ellis had used for a shield.

Pratt grinned. "I guess it's time we released the damsel in distress."

TWENTY-SIX

It took forty-eight hours to get Trudell in to make a statement. By that time she'd hired Walter Hodges, one of Toronto's best-known criminal lawyers. The irony was, she'd faced off against him in court many times—and tried her hardest to make him look bad.

"My client is just here to make a statement. I want to make that clear," Hodges said as they took seats in an interview room.

Pratt kept his face blank as he answered, "Of course."

He started up the recording unit, but Ellis opened his notebook nonetheless.

"Now," Pratt began, "tell us what happened."

Trudell drew herself up. It was odd to see her on the opposite side of the table in an interview room.

"Daniel Johnson set me up for that meeting at the courthouse yesterday."

"How?"

"I got an email."

"May I see it?"

Trudell and her lawyer huddled.

"You may not," Hodges answered.

Pratt sighed. Why did lawyers always make things so bloody difficult?

"So Johnson lured you to the provincial court building."

"Yes," Trudell said.

"Didn't you recognize him?"

"No. He had a beard—and I barely knew the man anyway."

"And what happened?"

"He called me by the name I used when I was young. He had a knife underneath the coat over his arm. He pushed it against my back and told me I had to come with him."

"Did you know why?"

"I could only guess that it had something to do with the trouble he got into eighteen years ago. He accused me and some of my friends of being involved in it. That was completely absurd."

"And after that, did he say anything else?"

"He spoke very little. With the point of a knife in my back, I had little choice but to go along with him."

"You knew what he'd done to your friends, didn't you?"

Another huddle, this time longer.

"My client wishes to say that she did know some of the other victims—"

"Not all of them?" Pratt shot back.

More talk.

"Well, yes. All of them. But Ms. Trudell hasn't spoken to any of them for many, many years. She lost touch with them once she went to university."

"We were never that close anyway," Trudell added. "I just hung out with them during the summers I spent at my aunt and uncle's cottage."

"And Daniel Johnson?"

"Just the kid who worked at the gas station. As I said before, I barely knew him and never spoke to him in my life."

Pratt switched gears. "Tell me why you left your childhood name completely behind."

"Detective Pratt," Hodges warned, "that has nothing to do with what happened yesterday."

Pratt ignored the lawyer. "Or why you've dyed your blond hair brown all these years. Most women would be thrilled to have blond hair."

"Detective! My client came here this morning to help with your investigation, not be subjected to baseless accusations. May I remind you she was nearly murdered two days ago?"

Pratt stared at Gwen Trudell for several moments. He had a hunch she was teetering.

Sliding an old photo across the table, he asked, "This is all six of you, isn't it?"

She picked it up, stared for a moment, then let it flutter from her fingers.

"Where did you get this?"

"From Bruce Moore's mother. It arrived by courier this morning. That's Curt Dewalt on the end, with his arm around you, then Becky Collins, Tom Lamport, Bruce Moore and Saara Lahti. Your hair is blond, strikingly so."

"We were so young."

Pratt said in a gentle voice, "We know what happened all those years ago."

"Hearsay," Hodges snapped.

"Maggie?"

Her head went down for nearly a minute. Then she finally looked up.

"I'm sorry, Walter, but I can't carry this burden any longer. I just can't." Another long pause. "Detective Pratt, ask me any question you want."

"Gwen!" Hodges said. "I cannot allow this."

She put her hand on the lawyer's forearm. "It's time to tell the truth, Walter. Way past time."

Pratt asked, "Why did you keep silent for so long?"

"I didn't think I would at first." She shook her head. "Despite what you may think of me, I'm not a bad person."

"How do you square that with ruining an innocent young man's life? You *and* your friends lied. Your parents lied. How could you allow that?"

"We panicked. Curt bolted into the woods, and we all followed. At least, *I* thought everyone followed. Bruce had a small flashlight. We stumbled around for hours. You wouldn't believe the shape we were in! Eventually, we came to a cottage. Tom knew the family who owned it. They gave us all rides back home. Bruce made up some stupid story about a boat with engine trouble."

"And when word got out about the accident?"

"Bruce's and Becky's parents figured out we were lying. They brought us all together, along with a lawyer from Toronto. It was made clear our lives would be ruined if what actually happened ever got out. Our parents swore us to secrecy, and we all got sent away. University was about to start up anyway.

"I kept wanting to tell. Curt was the one who really applied pressure on us to keep silent. He'd had trouble with the police back in Calgary, and that's why he'd been sent to Muskoka that summer. He told us he'd go to jail, and if that happened, he'd make sure we all went with him."

"So you kept silent."

Gwen Trudell squeezed her eyes shut. "Yes."

"I've looked at your biography online. Besides changing your name and hair color in order to hide your past, you have made no mention of all those summers in Muskoka. Do you even need those glasses you're wearing?"

Finally, the lawyer spoke up again.

"Gwen, you really have to stop." He looked at Pratt. "This interview is at an end."

Pratt turned off the recorder and got up.

"You disgust me," was all he said as he left the room.

Back in Mac's office, they discussed what would happen next.

"It's up to the Crown," Mac said. "There doesn't seem to be much stomach for looking deeper into this. If she hasn't already, Trudell will no doubt resign. Everyone else involved is dead."

Ellis shook his head. "What about Featherstone? I'm sure he was paid off, and there might be others. The parents represented a lot of power and money. You read the accounts of the case. It just screams of a setup."

Mac shrugged. "Not our call. I know it stinks, but it is what it is."

"It's a goddamn tragedy," Pratt said. "It amazes me what people will say to justify their actions. You expect better—but you never get it."

"Ain't that the truth, Pratt." Mac stood. "Well, boys, good work. I need the write-up on my desk ASAP."

TWENTY-SEVEN

Ellis was still fuming when he arrived home that evening. He wanted to go after Featherstone and had been told that wouldn't happen either.

When Jen had found out about what happened in the parking garage, she'd been as angry as he'd expected. Tonight she seemed quiet.

"Still mad?" he asked as they sat down to dinner.

"No." She looked up at him, eyes distant. "I have something to tell you."

Ellis's heart sank. He knew she'd been unhappy lately. Surely she couldn't want to leave him!

Then Jennifer laughed.

"You look so frightened!" She got up from her seat, came over and sat on his lap. "I wanted to tell you this morning, but you cleared out so quickly, I didn't have time."

"Tell me what?"

"First you have to promise to be much better about staying safe in the future."

"I'll quit my job if that's what it takes to make you happy."

"There's no need. I know you love being a cop." She kissed his forehead. "Do you promise?"

"Of course! Now what is it you want to tell me?"

"David Ellis, you're going to be a daddy."

Something is terribly wrong at Symphony Hall. Luigi Spadafini, the symphony's star conductor, has been murdered—and the entire orchestra has confessed to the crime. This is the mess that Detective Lieutenant Pratt walks into one Saturday morning. Overworked and tired, he's also saddled with Detective Ellis, the newest member of the homicide squad and still very wet behind the ears.

This is the first book in the Pratt and Ellis mystery series.

"A vibrant closed-room police procedural sure" to resonate with readers. —*Library Journal*

RAPID READS
WWW.RAPID-READS.COM

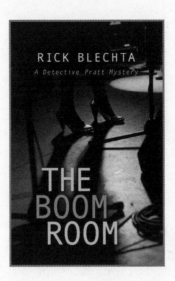

RICK BLECHTA
A Detective Pratt Mystery

THE
BOOM
ROOM

Detective Mervin Pratt is enjoying a quiet dinner at his favorite Italian restaurant when he's called in to assist at a murder scene at a popular downtown nightclub. The manager has been stabbed to death in his office.

When Pratt's young partner, Dave Ellis, arrives on the scene uninvited and quietly tells Pratt that the suspect is his half brother, Pratt finds himself in an ethical dilemma.

This is the second book in the Pratt and Ellis mystery series.

"The action picks up right away and "
there's never a lull. —*ForeWord*

RAPID READS
WWW.RAPID-READS.COM

RICK BLECHTA has two passions in life: music and writing. A professional musician since age fourteen, he often brings his extensive knowledge of that life to his crime fiction. Rick is now the author of three novellas for Orca, as well as eight novels. His novel *Cemetery of the Nameless* (2005) was shortlisted for the Arthur Ellis Best Novel Award, and his second Orca novella *The Boom Room* (2014) was shortlisted for the Arthur Ellis Best Novella Award. Rick participates in a blog called Type M for Murder, which can be found at www.typem4murder.blogspot.com. For more information about Rick, visit www.rickblechta.com.